This book is presented to

_____

on the occasion of

_____

by

_____

_____

Date

Dear Mommy

Nikki Rach

CPH
SAINT LOUIS

2 3 4 5 6 7 8 9 10   08   07   06   05   04   03   02   01   00

Contents

Preface

*I*t is my hope and prayer that this book will encourage you as you serve God as a mommy, wife, and godly woman. The responsibilities entrusted to women seem great at times. Beyond the dishes, laundry, and cleaning is our true calling—developing the character of our children, creating an atmosphere of love and growth, and nurturing the best in our husband and children. And God promises to provide more than we need or even imagine! He continually amazes me with moments of serendipity. Often God stops me and shows me His grace in the eyes, smiles, and tears of my children.

Writing this book posed three unique challenges for me. First was identifying what is helpful in raising godly children. With experts on every side declaring techniques that completely contradict one another, I often scratch my head in confusion. The next challenge rested in perceiving motherhood through the eyes of a child. What does a good mommy look like at knee level? Finally, the ongoing challenge lies in trying to live up to the letters. I do not claim to be an expert in raising children—this book is from the heart of a weary and wacky mom, who is passing on a few nuggets. I am certainly learning as I go along.

I have my husband to thank for all this. When I was a teenager, he encouraged me to be a Mega-W.O.G. That is a woman of God who strives to live a life worthy of the Gospel. When we married, he taught me what a godly home looks like. And of course, the children are blessings for which he is at least 50 percent responsible. Finally, in his endeavors to write a book, Dennis envisioned a book for daddies written from the perspective of a child. This is the companion book for mommies. I am quite indebted to my wonderful hubby for all the ways he has transformed my life and followed God's leading!

Then there are the real authors of the book—Jonathan and JuliAnne. Daily, they show me childlike faith. Daily they help me grow in patience and mercy. Daily they bring smiles to my face, laughter to my belly, and tears to my eyes! Being a mommy surpasses every image I had when the pregnancy test came back positive.

Finally, all praise and glory I lift to the Lord. He has richly blessed me with a wonderful husband and children. He has set before me countless role models—my mom, Connie Calub; her mom, Irene Ubben; my stepmother, Katherine Dunse; Anne Horne, and many more. Most important, He sustains me each day!

My prayer is that He sustain you as you strive to be the best mommy you can be.

Nikki

Being
a
Mother

He settles the barren
woman in her home
as a happy
mother of children.
Praise the LORD.

Psalm 113:9

A good mommy values her role.

Dear Mommy,

I know you sneak out of the house early in the morning to go rollerblading. I hope that helps, so we won't drive you crazy quite so quickly!

Love, JuliAnne

Dear Mommy,

I love the silly songs we sing as we clean up my toys. I think you're tricking me into doing my chores!

Love, Jonathan

Dear Mommy,

How do you keep it all together? Hunting for keys, tying shoes, wiping noses, changing diapers, and cleaning up toys—you must go crazy!

Love, JuliAnne

Dear Mommy,

I can hear you whistling while you work. I'm glad you have so much fun taking care of our home and our family.

Love, JuliAnne

Dear Mommy,

I love it when you whisper in my ear that you love me, especially when you seal it with a kiss!

Love, JuliAnne

Dear Mommy,

We spent the whole day in the car today! We had fun watching the tractors, police cars, and slug bugs. But I sure got wiggly from sitting still for so long. Maybe tomorrow we can spend more time playing!

Love, Jonathan

Dear Mommy,

I like having time with just you and me. When is our next girls' night out?

Love, JuliAnne

Dear Mommy,

I like helping you with the laundry. Thanks for letting me dangle my feet in the water while the washer is filling up.

Love, Jonathan

Dear Mommy,

Thanks for making me your big helper with JuliAnne. I like to get the diapers and wipes and to hold her bottle all by myself!

Love, Jonathan

Dear Mommy,

How did you learn how to cook all that yummy food? Will you teach me?

Love, JuliAnne

Dear Mommy,

Let's play the piano. I'll make some music and you clap at the end. Have you noticed that my songs keep getting shorter? That way you cheer more often!

Love, Jonathan

Dear Mommy,
    Thanks for taking a nap
with me this afternoon.
We both needed it!

    Love, Jonathan

10 Hints from Mommy

1. Cherish the role God has given you. It will be filled with many joys and struggles. Your attitude will make all the difference.

2. Look for the excitement in everyday life. There are many ways to make mundane chores fun.

3. When the children are driving you crazy and you want to disown them, find something fun to do together. A change of pace can do wonders for your attitude.

4. Exercise. It helps to balance out the emotional seesaw of motherhood.

5. Remember, you won't do everything right, but you also won't do everything wrong.

6. Take a break—you've earned it!

7. Make your own "happy hour," a time to do something that makes you happy. (It can even be nap time—yours or theirs!)

8. Laugh and love a lot.

9. You may never win a "Mother of the Year" award, but you will always be a hero to your children.

10. Seek support from other mothers. You are not the first mom to put a diaper on backward or to call the doctor six times in the first two weeks of your child's life.

Being
a
Great Wife

A wife of noble character
who can find?
She is worth far more than rubies.
Her husband has full confidence
in her and lacks nothing of value.

Proverbs 31:10–11

A good mommy
is a great wife.

Dear Mommy,

　It was fun looking through the pictures of your wedding. I almost didn't recognize Daddy with all that hair!

　　　　　　Love, Jonathan

Dear Mommy,

　We had fun playing with Aunt Sharon tonight when you and Daddy left. You must have had fun too, because you were both grinning really big. I'm glad you and Daddy like each other so much!

　　　　　　Love, JuliAnne

Dear Mommy,

　Why do you and Daddy hold hands? Are you afraid he will get lost?

　　　　　　Love, Jonathan

Dear Mommy,

I saw you writing a love letter to Daddy this morning. Why did you fill it with confetti?

Love, JuliAnne

Dear Mommy,

It sure is nice of you to make Daddy's favorite meal for dinner. Of course, he makes it easy since his favorite meal is pizza delivered to our house! That's my favorite meal too.

Love, Jonathan

Dear Mommy,

I heard you and Daddy working late on a project. You two giggle a lot when you work together. I'm sure Daddy appreciates your help.

Love, JuliAnne

Dear Mommy,

Why am I your second favorite guy in all the earth? Who's your most favorite? Daddy?

Love, Jonathan

Dear Mommy,
Isn't Daddy the greatest?!

Love, JuliAnne

Dear Mommy,
*   I think that at least one of*
you should take my side.
How's a kid supposed to get
ahead if you and Daddy
always take the same side?

Love, Jonathan

Dear Mommy,
*   You always have a hug for Daddy when he comes home.*
Some days they are longer than others. Does he have a
hug meter so that you know when he's running low?

Love, JuliAnne

Dear Mommy,
*   We had fun giving Daddy his tickle torture tonight.*
I never knew that playing "this little piggy" could be so
much fun!

Love, Jonathan

Dear Mommy,
    I like our early morning
time together. It's nice of us
to let Daddy sleep in, but
it's even more fun to pounce
on him and wake him up.
                Love, JuliAnne

10 Hints from Mommy

1. The best gift you can give your children is a loving relationship with their daddy.
2. Enjoy your husband.
3. Work out tough decisions before you bring them to the children. Let your children see a united front. If a problem arises between you and your husband, resolve it quickly.
4. If your husband comes home with two dozen roses, don't ask, "What did you get these for?" He may respond with, "Five bucks!"
5. Remember your priorities: God first, husband second, family third. The rest will take care of itself!
6. Lavish your husband with praise. It will bring out the best in him—and you.
7. Your children see their daddy as a hero. Do you?
8. Keep the fire of intimacy alive. Candlelight dinners and moonlit strolls don't have to be memories. It doesn't matter who initiates the romantic times together, you'll both enjoy them.
9. Write love letters to your husband often.
10. Remember, you were a wife before you were a mommy. After the children are on their own, it will be just the two of you again. Make the best of your time together as a family and as a couple.

Being
a
Woman of God

*Charm is deceptive,
and beauty is fleeting;
but a woman
who fears the LORD
is to be praised.*

Proverbs 31:30

*A good mommy
is a godly woman.*

Dear Mommy,

I love it when you sing Bible songs and put my name in them. It makes me feel snuggly all over!

Love, JuliAnne

Dear Mommy,

Thanks for letting me draw on our prayer board. Uncle Gary will never know that I drew a picture over his name, will he?

Love, Jonathan

Dear Mommy,

I have fun going with you to church for Bible study. I know the Bible is important to you because you take time to read it every day. Soon you will be able to teach me about the Bible!

Love, JuliAnne

Dear Mommy,

You told me that prayer is like a phone call to your best friend. You're happy to talk and be close to your friend. Can God be my friend too?

Love, JuliAnne

Dear Mommy,

It looks like you really like meeting with those ladies every week for "accountability." I thought by now all of you would know how to count!

Love, Jonathan

Dear Mommy,

I like all the Bible verses you have around the house. I can't wait to learn new ones with you. I think the ones on the steering wheel of the car help you the most!

Love, JuliAnne

Dear Mommy,

We had a great time singing Christmas carols to the shut-ins from church. If they are "shut-in," how come some of them weren't at home?

Love, Jonathan

Dear Mommy,

    It was neat to meet all the children at the shelter. I hope they liked the food I helped you cook.

                                                  Love, Jonathan

Dear Mommy,

    What's an arrow prayer? I think you hit me with one the other day!

                                                  Love, JuliAnne

Dear Mommy,

    Why do you like your quiet time so much? I love it noisy all the time! (Oh, maybe that's why!)

                                                  Love, Jonathan

Dear Mommy,

    I have fun playing in the nursery while you teach Sunday school. It will be fun to be in your class someday.

                                                  Love, JuliAnne

Dear Mommy,

Why did you get so upset when I drew a picture in your Bible? I see you write in it all the time!

Love, Jonathan

10 Hints from Mommy

1. Make God your first priority. You'll be a much better wife and mother when you are sure you are right with Christ first.

2. Keep a prayer list, and spend time in thoughtful prayer. If you can't carve out 15–30 minutes at the beginning of each day, perhaps you can find five minutes every couple of hours in the day.

3. Pray continually throughout the day. Shoot arrow prayers up to God as thoughts or situations arise that need your prayers.

4. Volunteer—you can even make it a family affair.

5. Learn to say no to projects you aren't passionate about.

6. Find a group of women who can support you and keep you on the right path. Meeting weekly to share joys, struggles, successes, and failures helps to smooth rough waters.

7. Dive into God's Word. Daily doses of Scripture keep you healthy and well-balanced.

8. Keep meaningful passages of Scripture in your heart, your head, and your house. They will serve as markers to help you maintain a walk of integrity.

9. Let your children see what you believe.

10. Start each day alone with the Lord.

Creating
Family
Traditions

*There, in the presence
of the LORD your God,
you and your families shall eat
and shall rejoice in everything
you have put your hand to,
because the LORD your God
has blessed you.*

Deuteronomy 12:7

*A good mommy creates
special family times.*

Dear Mommy,

    I like making cookies with you. It's especially fun to lick the spoon!

Love, Jonathan

Dear Mommy,

    I enjoy it when we do fun things together, all four of us. I really like it when we work together to help other people. I can't wait to see what we will be doing next month!

Love, JuliAnne

Dear Mommy,

    Who were all those people who kept patting my head and pinching my cheeks? It's fun to meet all those family members, but from my angle, all their knees look alike!

Love, Jonathan

Dear Mommy,

Thanks for taking me to Mama and Papa's house. I have so much fun chasing the cats, helping with chores at the farm, and running and playing. I especially like being with Mama and Papa. Thanks for sharing me with them and sharing them with me!

Love, Jonathan

Dear Mommy,

When will it be my turn to use the "you are special" plate at dinner?

Love, JuliAnne

Dear Mommy,

Will we be making our own Christmas presents again this year? We sure made a mess last year! But everyone really liked my reindeer!

Love, Jonathan

Dear Mommy,

I had fun with the egg toss at the family reunion. The best part was when the egg landed on you! I'm happy to be part of a family that is silly together.

Love, Jonathan

Dear Mommy,

    Thank you for rocking me each night. I didn't know all those songs had the same chorus, "Zzzzzz!"

Love, JuliAnne

Dear Mommy,

    It's time for our yearly trip to the photo studio. Can I wear my birthday suit? How about my swim suit?

Love, Jonathan

Dear Mommy,

    Why do I have to wait until Daddy reads the Christmas story before I can start opening my presents? Did he forget what happens?

Love, JuliAnne

Dear Mommy,

    I'll show JuliAnne the ropes for our Advent family devotions. I'll even make sure she doesn't put her fingers in the candles.

Love, Jonathan

Dear Mommy,

When can we chase the waves on the beach again? I hope the crabs won't eat my piggies!

Love, Jonathan

10 Hints from Mommy

1. Family traditions glue a family together and give it a unique identity.
2. Family traditions don't just happen; they require thoughtful preparation.
3. Create time to create memories together.
4. Your traditions should serve your family, not the other way around. If your family has outgrown a tradition, replace it with a more appropriate one.
5. A family tradition can be as simple as reading a book together each night or as elaborate as an annual vacation. The extent doesn't matter—the event does.
6. Children need *both* quality and quantity time.
7. Routine and repetition help solidify traditions. Don't be afraid to do some activities over and over again.
8. Develop family pride through unique activities and catchy phrases.
9. Family traditions should be fun—the sillier, the better.
10. Use holidays as opportunities to develop special family traditions.

Building Your Child's Self-Image

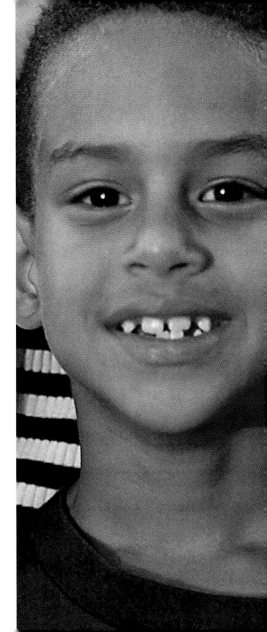

*To be made new
in the attitude
of your minds;
and to put on
the new self,
created to be like God
in true righteousness
and holiness.*

Ephesians 4:23–24

*A good mommy is crazy
about her children.
(Or is that crazy
because of her children?!)*

Dear Mommy,
I like the way we play soccer. I run and
kick and chase the ball, and you cheer for me!
Love, Jonathan

Dear Mommy,

    I like your kisses in the morning. But do you have to leave the lip prints?

Love, Jonathan

Dear Mommy,

    I like to hear you brag about me to other people. (Because I am advanced for my age, you know!)

Love, JuliAnne

Dear Mommy,

    Thank you for holding my hand when I try new things. Sometimes I just have to borrow your confidence.

Love, Jonathan

Dear Mommy,

    I know you love me. It's nice to know that you like me too!

Love, Jonathan

Dear Mommy,

    What's that one-eyed monster Daddy keeps putting in my face? Does saying cheeeeese make the bright light flash? Jonathan sure likes it.

                         Love, JuliAnne

Dear Mommy,

    If you think I'm so handsome, why did you pin a note to my chest that says, "My daddy dressed me"?

                         Love, Jonathan

Dear Mommy,

    Tell me again how proud you are of me.

                         Love, JuliAnne

Dear Mommy,

    Thank you for letting me play with my godparents. It's fun to see them looking through the window, waiting for me.

                         Love, Jonathan

Dear Mommy,

    Self, Mommy! I can do it by myself! (I think.)

Love, Jonathan

Dear Mommy,

    I like it when you clap and giggle with me. My droolly smile is almost as big as yours.

Love, JuliAnne

Dear Mommy,
   I like it when
we meet nose to nose
and your eyes sparkle
and the corners
   of your mouth turn
   into a giant grin.
   Love, JuliAnne

10 Hints from Mommy

1. A child requires love, hugs, and cheers to build self-confidence.
2. Make your ultimate goal to build up a child who loves God, knows His Word, and acts in a manner worthy of the Gospel.
3. Your child needs people in his life who are crazy about him. Are you?
4. Our greatest source of self-worth comes from knowing Jesus' love for us. Help your child experience her incredible value and worth as a child of God.
5. Challenge your child to try new things—food, activities, chores, etc.
6. Share your children with others. A large web of positive relationships will provide a strong safety net in tough times.
7. If your child feels secure in your relationship with his daddy, he will have more courage to grow and try new things.
8. Avoid comparing your child to other children or siblings.
9. Catch your child doing things right, then reinforce that behavior.
10. Let your child see your love for her in your eyes.

Instilling
Positive
Values

*These commandments
that I give you today
are to be upon your hearts.
Impress them on your children.
Talk about them
when you sit at home and
when you walk along the road,
when you lie down
and when you get up.*

Deuteronomy 6:6–7

*A good mommy plants
seeds of faith daily.*

Dear Mommy,

I'm sorry! Will you forgive me?

Love, JuliAnne

Dear Mommy,

It sure is fun to make cards and pictures for other people. The best part is to see them smile when they open the cards!

Love, Jonathan

Dear Mommy,

It's hard to learn how to share, but I like sharing my banana with you. I get the banana and you get the peel!

Love, Jonathan

Dear Mommy,

I like going to church with you and Daddy and hearing all the pretty music. I don't understand everything you do in there, but I sure like being at God's house!

Love, JuliAnne

Dear Mommy,

Why did Pastor Mike sprinkle water on JuliAnne's head? If she's a child of God now, why do we have to watch her? Are you God's baby sitter?

Love, Jonathan

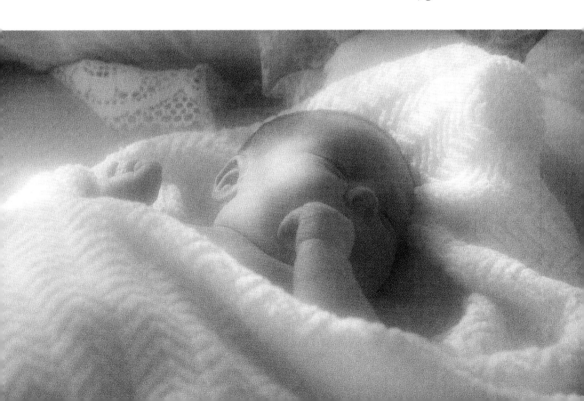

Dear Mommy,

I like it when our family kneels around the altar and the pastor pats me on the head and says God loves me. When will I be able to have a snack up there with you?

Love, JuliAnne

Dear Mommy,

I like to sit in your lap and "read" along with you and Pastor in the Bible. How come the church Bibles don't have any pictures?

Love, Jonathan

Dear Mommy,

I don't like to be patient! When I'm hungry, I want to eat! Do I have to wait until everyone else is at the table and we pray before I start eating?

Love, JuliAnne

Dear Mommy,

I feel like a big boy when I can pray with you and Daddy. Remember to slow down a little so I can keep up!

Love, Jonathan

Dear Mommy,

How does God know if I put my 50 cents in the offering plate or the soda machine?

Love, Jonathan

Dear Mommy,

   It was great to see you give back the extra money the cashier gave you. (Even though it was going to go to join the other quarters in my college fund!)

Love, JuliAnne

Dear Mommy,

   Thank you for thanking me for following directions.

Love, Jonathan

10 Hints from Mommy

1. Incorporate your child in your daily walk with Christ.
2. Teach your child your prayers.
3. Worship together as a family, even when it gets crazy.
4. Live your faith and your children will learn it.
5. Serve others in need together as a family. It not only will bond your family but also will teach your children values.
6. Values are caught, not taught.
7. Even when you think no one is watching, little eyes may be peering at you. Act like you want your children to act.
8. Look for teachable moments and take advantage of them.
9. Praise your children for little things—children learn more from affirmation and praise than from criticism.
10. Have reasons for your rules and share them with your children. If they know the reason behind the rule, they can think through the right way to act in new situations.

Having Fun

I know that
there is nothing
better for men
than to be happy
and do good
while they live.

Ecclesiastes 3:12

*A good mommy has a
blast with her family.*

Dear Mommy,

 Thanks for taking me to the park for a picnic lunch. I love to run and play and jump, especially with you.

Love, Jonathan

Dear Mommy,

 It's fun to play hide and seek with Jonathan. What would happen if we didn't find him?

Love, JuliAnne

Dear Mommy,

 Let's splash around in the pool again!

Love, Jonathan

Dear Mommy,

 Why do you chant, "Water, water, water!" while Daddy tees off at miniature golf? I don't think it helps!

Love, JuliAnne

Dear Mommy,
    Let's run outside
and play in the
sprinklers again.
        Love, Jonathan

Dear Mommy,

    Let's make JuliAnne surf on your water bed again.

Love, Jonathan

Dear Mommy,

    I like it when you copy me. Your raspberries sure sound silly!

Love, JuliAnne

Dear Mommy,

    The lizards and butterflies need to slow down. I can't catch them when they run so fast!

Love, Jonathan

Dear Mommy,

I liked doing the dishwasher dance. It's a good thing we didn't break any of those dishes!

Love, Jonathan

10 Hints from Mommy

1. The family that plays together stays together.
2. Get crazy with your kids.
3. Watch your child discover his world and capture his sense of wonder.
4. Adventure lies just around the corner, in the cabinet, or under the crib. Look for it.
5. Get out of the house and go exploring.
6. Family fun doesn't need to cost a lot—parks, pools, and restaurants offer great, free places to play.
7. If you run out of ideas, ask a preschool teacher for simple songs or games you can play at home.
8. Add fun to the mundane chores of the day.
9. Be quick to laugh, especially at yourself.
10. When you find something that works for your child or family, capitalize on it.